THE BIG RACE

D1102675

DAVID BARROW

LANCASHIRE COUNTY LIBRARY
30118137360461

The Big Race was very tough.

Only the **fastest, biggest** and **strongest** animals could take part.

"I'd like to enter please," said little Aardvark.

"What? You?" said Lion. "You'll never finish."

"Oh, yes I will!" said Aardvark.

THE BIG
RACE
ENTRY
FORM

Cheetah was very **fast**.
Buffalo was very **big**.
And Crocodile was
very **strong**.

"You'll never finish!"
they sniggered.

"I will, and
I'll have fun,"
said Aardvark.

The animals lined up at the start. It was going to be the race of their lives.

Warthog called out:

"On your
marks ...
get set ...

... go!" They charged across the dusty desert.

Cheetah was in the lead ...

Buffalo was close behind ...

and Crocodile **too!**

Aardvark was hot on their heels.

They cycled up the hill.
Buffalo pushed into first place ...
Crocodile puffed into second place ...
and Cheetah slipped into third place.
Aardvark was close behind.

They plunged down the waterfall.

Buffalo did
backstroke ...

Cheetah did a
cannonball ...

and Crocodile dived
in head first.

"Whee!!" laughed Aardvark.

The animals swam **under** the water ...

and wobbled **over** the valley.

Aardvark was very tired.

But she'd never give up.

The others **powered** onwards
through the woods ...

and upwards into the air.

The Big Race was
almost over.

"Maybe the other
animals were right."
sighed Aardvark.
Perhaps I'll never finish."

Then all of a sudden ...

PC

DPI

Aardvark tumbled down
through the air ...

past Buffalo ...

past Cheetah ...

past Crocodile ...

and landed safely almost
at the finish line.

But the others were
coming up behind her ...

Would Aardvark make it?

WHOOSH!

Cheetah, Buffalo and Crocodile couldn't agree on who had crossed the finish line first.

But Aardvark had shown everyone that you don't need to be the fastest, biggest or strongest to join in and have fun.

She **did finish** the Big Race.
And she got a medal.

"**Hooray** for Aardvark," all her friends cheered.

For Martin and Pam. This is all their fault.

Big thanks to Sam.

HODDER CHILDREN'S BOOKS
First published in Great Britain in 2018 by Hodder and Stoughton
Text and illustration copyright © David Barrow, 2018

The moral rights of the author and illustrator have been asserted.
All rights reserved
A CIP catalogue record for this book is available from the British Library.
HB ISBN: 978 1 444 92928 7
PB ISBN: 978 1 444 92929 4
1 3 5 7 9 10 8 6 4 2
Printed and bound in China
Hodder Children's Books, an imprint of Hachette Children's Group,
part of Hodder and Stoughton
Carmelite House, 50 Victoria Embankment, London, EC4Y 0DZ
An Hachette UK Company
www.hachette.co.uk
www.hachettechildrens.co.uk